KU-543-446

HORRID HENRY
and the **Football Fiend**

HORRiD HENRY
and the **Football Fiend**

Francesca Simon
Illustrated by Tony Ross

Orion
Children's Books

Horrid Henry and the Football Fiend originally appeared in
Horrid Henry and the Football Fiend first published in Great Britain
in 2006 by Orion Children's Books
This edition first published in Great Britain in 2010
by Orion Children's Books
a division of the Orion Publishing Group Ltd
Orion House
5 Upper Saint Martin's Lane
London WC2H 9EA
An Hachette UK Company

Text © Francesca Simon 2006
Illustrations © Tony Ross 2010

The right of Francesca Simon and Tony Ross to be identified
as author and illustrator of this work has been asserted.

All rights reserved. No part of this publication may be
reproduced, stored in a retrieval system, or transmitted,
in any form or by any means, electronic, mechanical,
photocopying, recording or otherwise, without the prior
permission of Orion Children's Books.

The Orion Publishing Group's policy is to use papers that
are natural, renewable and recyclable products and made
from wood grown in sustainable forests. The logging and
manufacturing processes are expected to conform to the
environmental regulations of the country of origin.

A catalogue record for this book is available from the British Library.

Printed by C&C Offset Printing Co., Ltd, China

www.orionbooks.co.uk
www.horridhenry.co.uk

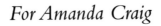

For Amanda Craig

Look out for . . .

Don't Be Horrid, Henry!
Horrid Henry's Birthday Party
Horrid Henry's Holiday
Horrid Henry's Underpants
Horrid Henry Gets Rich Quick

Contents

Chapter 1

"…AND with 15 seconds to go
it's Hot-Foot Henry racing across
the pitch!

Rooney tries a slide tackle
but Henry's too quick!

Just look at that step-over!

Oh no, he can't score from
that distance,

it's **crazy**,

it's **impossible**,

oh my goodness,
he cornered the ball. . .

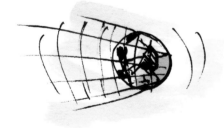

it's IN!!!! It's IN!

Another spectacular win!
And it's all thanks to Hot-Foot
Henry, the greatest footballer
who's ever lived!"

"Goal! Goal! Goal!"
roared the crowd.

Hot-Foot Henry had won the match!
His teammates carried him through
the fans, cheering and chanting,
"Hen-ry! Hen-ry! Hen-ry!"

"HENRY!"

Horrid Henry looked up to see Miss
Battle-Axe leaning over his table and
glaring at him with her red eyes.
"What did I just say?"

"Henry," said Horrid Henry.
Miss Battle-Axe scowled.
"I'm watching you, Henry," she
snapped. "Now class, please pay
attention, we need to discuss—"

"Waaaaa!"
wailed Weepy William.

"Susan, stop pulling
my hair!"
squealed Vain Violet.

"Miss!"
shouted Inky Ian.
"Ralph's snatched
my pen!"

"Didn't!"
shouted Rude Ralph.

"Did!"
shouted Inky Ian.

"Class! Be quiet!"
bellowed Miss Battle-Axe.

"Waaaaa!"

wailed Weepy William.

"OWWWW!"

squealed Vain Violet.

"Give it back!"

shouted Inky Ian.

"Fine," said Miss Battle-Axe,
"we won't talk about football."

William stopped wailing.
Violet stopped squealing.
Ian stopped shouting.
Henry stopped daydreaming.

Everyone in the class stared at
Miss Battle-Axe.

Chapter 2

Miss Battle-Axe wanted to talk about
… football?
Was this an alien Miss Battle-Axe?

"As you all know, our local team,
Ashton Athletic, has reached the
sixth round of the FA Cup,"
said Miss Battle-Axe.
"YAY!" shrieked the class.

"And I'm sure you all know what
happened last night…"

Last night!

Henry could still hear the
announcer's glorious words as
he and Peter had gathered round
the radio as the draw for
round six was announced.

"Number 16, Ashton Athletic, will be playing…" There was a long pause as the announcer drew another ball from the hat… "number 7, Manchester United."
"Go Ashton!" shrieked Horrid Henry.

"As I was saying, before I was so rudely interrupted…"
Miss Battle-Axe glared at Horrid Henry.

"Ashton are playing Manchester United in a few weeks. Every local primary school has been given a pair of tickets. And thanks to my good luck in the teachers' draw, the lucky winner will come from our class."

"Me!" screamed Horrid Henry.
"Me!" screamed Moody Margaret.
"Me!" screamed Tough Toby,
Aerobic Al, Fiery Fiona and
Brainy Brian.

"No one who shouts out
will be getting anything," said Miss
Battle-Axe. "Our class will be playing
a football match at lunchtime.
The player of the match will win
the tickets. I'm the referee and my
decision will be final."

Chapter 3

Horrid Henry was so stunned that for a moment he could scarcely breathe. FA Cup tickets! FA Cup tickets to see his local team Ashton play against Man U! Those tickets were like gold dust.

Henry had begged and pleaded
with Mum and Dad to get tickets,
but naturally they were all sold out
by the time Henry's mean, horrible,
lazy parents managed to heave their
stupid bones to the phone.

And now here was another chance
to go to the match of the century!

Ashton Athletic had never got
so far in the Cup.
Sure, they'd knocked out the

Tooting Tigers
(chant: Toot Toot! Grrr!),

the **Pynchley Pythons**
and the **Cheam Champions**

but – Manchester United!

Henry had to go to the game.
He just had to. And all he had to do
was be man of the match.

There was just one problem.
Unfortunately, the best footballer
in the class wasn't

Horrid Henry.

Or Aerobic Al.

Or Beefy Bert.

The **best footballer** in the class was Moody Margaret.

The **second best** player in the class was Moody Margaret.

The **third best** player in the class was Moody Margaret.

It was so unfair!

Why should Margaret of all people
be so fantastic at football?

Horrid Henry was brilliant
at shirt pulling.

Horrid Henry was superb
at screaming "Offside!"
(whatever that meant).

No one could howl
"Come on, ref!" louder.

And at

toe-treading,

 elbowing,

barging,

pushing,

shoving

and

tripping,

Horrid Henry had no equal.

The only thing Horrid Henry wasn't good at was playing football.

35

But never mind.
Today would be different.
Today he would dig deep inside
and find the power to be

Hot-Foot Henry

– for real.
Today no one would stop him.
FA Cup match here I come,
thought Henry gleefully.

Chapter 4

Lunchtime!

Horrid Henry's class dashed to
the back playground where the pitch
was set up. Two jumpers either end
marked the goals. A few parents
gathered on the sidelines.

Miss Battle-Axe split the class into
two teams: Aerobic Al was captain of
Henry's team, Moody Margaret was
captain of the other.

There she stood in midfield, having
nabbed a striker position, smirking
confidently. Horrid Henry glared at
her from the depths of the outfield.

"Na na ne nah nah,

I'm sure to be man of the match,"
trilled Moody Margaret,
sticking out her tongue at him.
"and you-ooo won't."

"Shut up, Margaret," said Henry.
When he was king, anyone named
Margaret would be boiled in oil
and fed to the crows.

"Will you take me to the match,
Margaret?" said Susan.
"After all, *I'm* your best friend."
Moody Margaret scowled.
"Since when?"
"Since always!" wailed Susan.
"Huh!" said Margaret.
"We'll just have to see how nice
you are to me, won't we?"

"Take me,"

begged Brainy Brian.

"Remember how I helped you
with those fractions?"

" And called me **stupid**,"

said Margaret.

"Didn't," said Brian.

"Did," said Margaret.

Horrid Henry eyed his classmates.
Everyone looking straight ahead,
everyone determined to be man
of the match.

Well, wouldn't they be in for a shock when Horrid Henry waltzed off with those tickets!

Chapter 5

"Go Margaret!"

screeched
Moody Margaret's mum.

"Go Al!"

screeched
Aerobic Al's dad.

"Everyone ready?" said
Miss Battle-Axe.
"Bert! Which team are you on?"

"I dunno," said Beefy Bert.

Miss Battle-Axe blew her whistle.

Kick-off!

Kick.

Chase.

Kick.

Dribble.

Dribble.

Pass.

Kick.

Save!

Goal kick.

Henry stood disconsolately on the
left wing, running back and forth
as the play passed him by.
How could he ever be man of the
match stuck out here? Well, no way
was he staying in this stupid spot
a moment longer.

Horrid Henry abandoned his
position and chased after the ball.
All the other defenders followed him.

Moody Margaret had the ball.
Horrid Henry ran up behind her.

He glanced at Miss Battle-Axe.
She was busy chatting to
Mrs Oddbod.
Horrid Henry went for a two foot
slide tackle and tripped her.

Foul!
He hacked my leg!

Liar!
I just went for
the ball!

"Cheater!"
screamed Moody Margaret's
mum.

"Play on,"
ordered Miss Battle-Axe.
Yes! thought Henry triumphantly.
After all, what did blind old
Miss Battle-Axe know about
the rules of football?

Nothing.

This was his golden chance to score.
Now Jazzy Jim had the ball.

Horrid Henry trod on his toes,
elbowed him, and grabbed the ball.

"Hey, we're on the same team!"
yelped Jim.
Horrid Henry kept dribbling.
"Pass! Pass!" screamed Al. "Man on!"

Henry ignored him. Pass the ball?
Was Al mad? For once Henry had
the ball and he was keeping it.

Then suddenly Moody Margaret
appeared from behind, barged him,
dribbled the ball past Henry's team
and kicked it straight past
Weepy William into goal.

Moody Margaret's team cheered.
Weepy William burst into tears.

"Waaaaaa,"

wailed Weepy William.

"Idiot!"

screamed Aerobic Al's dad.

"She cheated!
She fouled me!"

shrieked Henry.

"Didn't,"

said Margaret.

"How dare you call my
daughter a cheater?" screamed
Moody Margaret's mum.

Miss Battle-Axe blew her whistle.
"Goal to Margaret's team.
The score is one-nil."

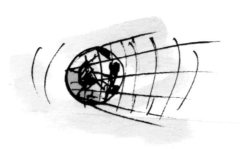

Chapter 6

Horrid Henry gritted his teeth.
He would score a goal if he had to
trample on every player to do so.
Unfortunately, everyone else seemed
to have the same idea.

"Ralph pushed me!"
shrieked Aerobic Al.
"Didn't," lied Rude Ralph.
"It was just a barge."

"He used his hands, I saw him!"
howled Al's father. "Send him off."
"I'll send *you* off if you don't
behave," snapped Miss Battle-Axe,
looking up and blowing her whistle.

"It was kept in!"
protested Henry.

"No way!" shouted Margaret.
"It went past the line!"

"That was ball to hand!"
yelled Kind Kasim.

"No way!" screamed Aerobic Al.
"I just went for the ball."

"Free kick to Margaret's team,"
said Miss Battle-Axe.
"Ouch!" screamed Soraya, as Brian
stepped on her toes, grabbed the ball,
and headed it into goal past Kasim.

"Hurray!" cheered Al's team.
"Foul!" screamed Margaret's team.

"Score is one all," said Miss
Battle-Axe. "Five more minutes
to go."

AAARRRGGHH!

thought Horrid Henry.
I've got to score a goal to have
a chance to be man of the match.
I've just got to. But how, how?

Henry glanced at Miss Battle-Axe. She appeared to be rummaging in her handbag.

Henry saw his chance. He stuck out his foot as Margaret hurtled past.

Crash!

Margaret tumbled.
Henry seized the ball.

Henry hacked my leg!

Did not! I just went for the ball.

"REF!"

screamed Margaret.

"He cheated!" screamed Margaret's mum. "Are you blind, ref?"

Miss Battle-Axe glared.
"My eyesight is perfect, thank you,"
she snapped.
Tee hee, chortled Horrid Henry.

Henry trod on Brian's toes, elbowed
him, then grabbed the ball.

Then Dave elbowed Henry,
Ralph trod on Dave's toes, and
Susan seized the ball and kicked it
high overhead.

Henry looked up.
The ball was high, high up.
He'd never reach it, not unless,
unless—

Henry glanced at Miss Battle-Axe.
She was watching a traffic warden
patrolling outside the school gate.
Henry leapt into the air and whacked
the ball with his hand.

Thwack!

The ball hurled across the goal.

"Goal!" screamed Henry.

"He used his hands!"
protested Margaret.

"No way!" shouted Henry.
"It was the hand of God!"

"Hen-ry! Hen-ry! Hen-ry!"

cheered his team.

"Unfair!"

howled Margaret's team.

Miss Battle-Axe blew her whistle.
"Time!" she bellowed.
"Al's team wins 2-1."
"Yes!" shrieked Horrid Henry,
punching the air. He'd scored the
winning goal! He'd be man of the
match! Ashton Athletic versus
Man U here I come!

Horrid Henry's class limped
through the door and sat down.
Horrid Henry sat at the front,
beaming.

Miss Battle-Axe had to award him
the tickets after his brilliant
performance and spectacular,
game-winning goal.

The question was, who *deserved*
to be his guest?

No one.

I know, thought Horrid Henry,
I'll sell my other ticket. Bet I get
a million pounds for it. No,
a billion pounds.

Then I'll buy my own football team,
and play striker any time I want to.
Horrid Henry smiled happily.

Miss Battle-Axe glared at her class. "That was absolutely disgraceful," she said. "Cheating! Moving the goals! Shirt tugging!"
She glared at Graham. "Barging!"
She glowered at Ralph. "Pushing and shoving! Bad sportsmanship!"

Her eyes swept over the class. Horrid Henry sank lower in his seat.

Oops.

"And don't get me started about offside," she snapped.

Horrid Henry sank even lower.
"There was only one person
who deserved to be player of the
match," she continued.
"One person who observed the rules
of the beautiful game…
One person who has nothing
to be ashamed of today…"

Horrid Henry's heart leapt.
He certainly had nothing
to be ashamed of.

"…One person who can truly
be proud of their performance…"
Horrid Henry beamed with pride.
"And that person is—"

"Me!"
screamed Moody Margaret.

"Me!"
screamed Aerobic Al.

"Me!"
screamed Horrid Henry.

"—the referee," said Miss Battle-Axe.

What?

Miss Battle-Axe ... man of the match?

Miss Battle-Axe ... a football fiend?

"IT'S NOT FAIR!"
screamed the class.

"IT'S NOT FAIR!"
screamed Horrid Henry.

More HORRID HENRY

Colour Books
Horrid Henry's Big Bad Book
Horrid Henry's Wicked Ways
Horrid Henry's Evil Enemies
Horrid Henry Rules the World
Horrid Henry's House of Horrors
Horrid Henry's Dreadful Deeds

Activity Books
Horrid Henry's Brainbusters
Horrid Henry's Headscratchers
Horrid Henry's Mindbenders
Horrid Henry's Colouring Book
Horrid Henry's Puzzle Book
Horrid Henry's Sticker Book
Horrid Henry's Mad Mazes
Horrid Henry's Wicked Wordsearches
Horrid Henry's Crazy Crosswords
Horrid Henry's Classroom Chaos
Horrid Henry's Holiday Havoc
Horrid Henry Runs Riot